Fierce Milly

and the demon saucepan

Also by
Marilyn McLaughlin:

Winner of the Bisto Eilís Dillon Award
and a Bisto Merit Award

(Red Banana)

Fierce Milly and the demon Saucepan

Marilyn McLaughlin

Illustrated by Leonie Shearing

EGMONT

To Gerry

First published in Great Britain in 2002
by Egmont Books Limited,
239 Kensington High Street, London, W8 6SA

ISBN 1 4052 0064 2

A CIP catalogue record for this book is available from the British Library

Printed in Great Britain by Cox & Wyman Ltd, Reading, Berkshire

Contents

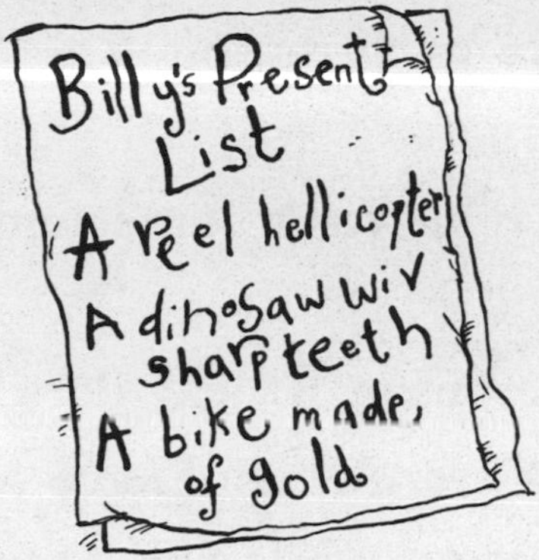

1.

Fierce Milly and the best birthday ever!

Billy was making lists for his birthday. The first list was who he wanted to come. Billy wrote: Fierce Milly and Susan and Yo-yo Ferguson.

'Are you sure about Fierce Milly?' Mum said. 'You know how loud she is.'

'She's our best friend,' Billy said. 'Nothing's any fun without her.'

'Does Yo-yo Ferguson *have* to come?' Mum asked.

'Fierce Milly won't come without him,' Billy said.

Yo-yo Ferguson is next door's new cat but he goes everywhere Fierce Milly goes. Nobody knows why. She scares all the other dogs and cats just by looking at them. She scares the babies in the prams just by smiling at them. Sometimes she even scares horrible Cecil Nutt and he's nearly a big boy.

'Oh well,' Mum said. 'I'll just get some cat food for him.'

'With a candle on it,' Billy said.

'What about wee Bertie that sits beside you in school?' Mum asked.

'Oh Mum,' I said, 'not wee Bertie! Ursula out of my class would have to come too. She's his big sister and he won't go anywhere without her.'

'He's silly,' Billy said.

'You're just the same,' I said. 'Last year I had to go to wee Bertie's party with you.'

'Then they both must come,' Mum said.

'There'll be Trouble if Ursula comes,' I said.

'There'll be no trouble,' Mum said. 'Ursula's a lovely nice quiet girl.'

Then Billy showed Mum his list of all the presents he wanted. She scored off all the scary things and all the impossible things and all the things that would cost a million pounds.

'It's going to be the best birthday ever,' Billy said.

By the time it got to Billy's birthday he was so excited that he was sick seven times before breakfast. Mum sent him back to bed with a basin.

When Fierce Milly called for us to go to school she asked, 'Are we still having the party?'

'Oh yes,' Mum said. 'Maybe Billy will be better by tea time.'

'I hope not,' Fierce Milly whispered. 'More cake for me!'

Then she said to Mum, 'If he's not any better we can trampoline on his bed, and that'll cheer him up.'

'Oh,' Mum said, with that worried look she gets around Fierce Milly, 'I hope it

won't be that sort of party.'

On the way to school, Fierce Milly asked, 'Who's coming to Billy's party then?'

I knew she was dividing up the cake in her head to see how much she'd get.

'You and me and Billy – if he stops being sick. And Mum. And maybe Dad – if he's home from work on time – and wee Bertie that sits beside Billy in school and Ursula from our class.'

I rushed the last bit hoping Fierce Milly wouldn't hear it, but she hears everything.

'Ursula! What *for*?'

'My mum says she has to come.'

'If she's going, I'm not going.'

'But you've got to come,' I said. 'It won't be the best birthday ever without you.'

Then the school bell rang and we had to run on into class. I know why Fierce Milly doesn't like Ursula. It's because Ursula's news always gets picked for the blackboard. Miss never picks Fierce Milly's news. Today she picked mine, so what went up on the board was: 'Poor Billy is sick on his birthday. Happy Birthday Billy, and Get Well Soon.'

Then it was time for multiplying. Fierce Milly loves multiplying and once she starts she doesn't stop. She multiplies over and over again, and when the numbers get too big

for her page, she multiplies all over my page as well, and last week she multiplied right on over the desk and on down to the floor and up the wall before Miss noticed.

Today Miss made her do her multiplying on big old sheets of painting paper, all spread out on the floor at the back of the class. Miss said, 'Now remember, Mildred, each number once only!' But you could tell by the rustling of big paper at the back of the room that Fierce Milly had forgotten about 'once only'.

When Miss said time to stop, Fierce Milly shouted, 'Miss, Miss, Miss. I got 5,419,921,875,000,000. That's the biggest number in the world! I want a star!'

Miss sighed, 'Yes dear, it is a very big number. But it's not the right one. Now Ursula, why don't you tell us the right number. I'm sure you did what you were supposed to.'

And then Ursula got a star.

'That's not fair,' Fierce Milly said. 'I did the most multiplying!'

Miss cut Fierce Milly's enormous number out of the big paper with scissors and taped it all together. That cheered Fierce Milly up. It was the longest number yet. She rolled it up, round and round like a swiss roll and put it on the desk. I kidnapped it.

'You can't have your number back until you promise to come to Billy's birthday.'

'I'll come. Give me my number back.'

'You can only come if you promise to be nice to Ursula. No Trouble!'

'Nice to Ursula?' She went pale and her mouth fell open.

'How about nearly nice?' I asked.

'The whole time?' she asked.

'The whole time she's at Billy's party.'

She looked relieved. 'Oh that's OK. I can do that.'

I gave her her number back. She put it in her pocket.

After school I ran all the way home to

see if Billy's birthday tea was ready. It was great. There were three colours of jelly, and meringues with cream, and baby sausage rolls, and marshmallow top hats, and sausages on sticks and chocolate crispy squares, and two types of sandwiches, and everything. And Billy was OK too. He hadn't been sick for ages and he was allowed out of bed again.

'Do you think it's enough, Susan?' Mum said. 'You know what a big appetite Fierce Milly has.'

Then the doorbell rang. It was Fierce

Milly and Yo-yo Ferguson. Fierce Milly had a huge present for Billy.

'Open it first, open it first!' she said, and she opened it herself. It was an enormous book, nearly as big as Billy.

It was called *Mighty Monsters of the Universe* and there was a vampire with too many teeth, snarling on the cover.

'Nice smile,' Billy said.

Fierce Milly said, 'I might be a vampire, when I grow up. But it's OK, I'll just have orange juice in the meantime.'

'What's a vampire?' Billy asked.

'Drinks blood,' Fierce Milly said.

I had my hands over Billy's ears just in time to stop him hearing that.

'Don't you dare scare our Billy on his birthday,' I said.

'Look at that food!' Fierce Milly yelled. 'Let me at it.'

'No-No-NO,' Mum said, holding her back by her belt. 'We have to wait for the others.'

Then the doorbell rang and it was Ursula and wee Bertie. Ursula was wearing a lovely new pink party frock.

She showed off, 'You haven't got a lovely new pink party frock. You haven't got matching pink socks *and* matching pink frilly knickers.'

I was so jealous I couldn't speak.

'Yeuch, pink! Bleurch! . . .' Fierce Milly started.

'Remember your promise,' I hissed. 'No Trouble!'

Fierce Milly smiled. It was a terrible smile, the sort that makes you shiver all over. 'Nice frock,' she said. I breathed a sigh of relief.

Mum said, 'Time for tea.'

We all charged in for the food. We had to eat very fast. Fierce Milly ate all the sausages on sticks. Yo-yo Ferguson ate the sticks. Then Yo-yo ate Fierce Milly's red jelly, and she yelled at him and said she was going to make a cat-disappearing-spell. Mum said she knew the best cat-disappearing-spell and she put Yo-yo out the back door. But he came in again through the kitchen window. That's why he's called Yo-yo. He keeps coming back.

Then Mum said, 'Why don't we play the party games?' So we started with Pass the Parcel and Pinning the Tail on the Donkey, and then telling the funniest joke and laughing the loudest, and then making the rudest noise, and then jumping off the sofa, and then trying to stand on our heads, and then Fierce Milly wanted to play trampolining on Ursula, but Mum wouldn't let her, and then Ursula felt sick because of all the being upside down, and Mum said it was time for everyone to go home, and then Mum said, 'Never again' and went upstairs for a little lie down.

At bedtime I said to Billy to leave *Mighty Monsters of the Universe* in my room, in case the monsters made him afraid in the night.

But he said that things in books were OK, because you can always shut the book. And things can't get out. They're stuck in the pictures. It's things *not* in books that are the problem. Then he tucked the book up in bed beside him and said it was the best birthday present ever. And I said that the most amazing thing of all was Fierce Milly being nearly nice to Ursula for a whole two hours. That was a record.

2.

Fierce Milly and the vampire granny

Fierce Milly really really wants Miss to pick her news for the blackboard. Everyone else just has news happen to them but Fierce Milly makes her news up. It's always something amazing, like there's mermaids down the grating beside Tony's shop, or she has a frog in her tummy because she drank Billy's tadpole by accident. But no matter how hard Fierce Milly tries, her news never gets picked. This was her news this morning:

'My granny's a vampire. I found her false vampire teeth in her sideboard drawer. She puts them in at night and changes into a bat and flies out the window and bites people, and I think I'm changing into a vampire too, because I looked at my teeth in the mirror this morning and they're getting longer and sharper and soon I'll be able to bite people, though I don't know when I'll be able to fly out the window like a bat.'

She opened her mouth big as a bucket and we all had a good look at her teeth. Even Miss got up to look. Some people thought the teeth were just the same as always. Other people thought they were definitely getting pointy and Ursula got scared. Then Miss clapped her hands and

said for everybody to stop being so silly, there are no such things as vampires, and Fierce Milly is most definitely *not* changing into one and had anybody got any sensible news?

After school Fierce Milly was still scolding, 'Why's it always boring old news gets picked? My news is the best. She should pick my news.'

'She doesn't pick your news because news has to be true. That's what news is about – things that really happen,' I said.

'But my news *is* true. My granny *is* a vampire. You come to her house and I'll show you her vampire false teeth.'

Billy said, 'Cool, false teeth are great.' He likes our granny's false teeth, because when they're in the glass of water beside her bed, he thinks they're smiling.

'Call for me after tea,' she said.

'Her granny's not a vampire,' I said, after she had gone. 'Nobody's granny is a vampire.'

'You never know with grannies,' Billy said.

Billy brought his *Mighty Monsters of the Universe* book with him, when we went to Fierce Milly's granny's, to look up vampires, seeing as we might be about to meet one. He read and walked at the same time. I steered him by the back of his collar.

'Does your granny sleep hanging upside down from the ceiling?' he asked.

'I've only ever seen her sleeping in her rocking chair and she was right way up then,' she said.

When we got to Fierce Milly's granny's house, Billy and Fierce Milly crowded up tight on the doorstep to be the first to see the vampire teeth. I stayed at the back in case she was a Fierce Granny. I didn't know which would be worse, Fierce or Vampire. When Fierce Milly's granny saw her she gave a great big smile. Not a lot of people smile when they see Fierce Milly. It was a good chance to have a real close look at her teeth. They were just ordinary. I knew they would be.

'Come on in and I'll make us all a cup of tea,' she said.

She told us to wait in the sitting-room.

'Where's these vampire teeth then?' Billy asked.

'Over here,' Fierce Milly said, and she opened a drawer in the sideboard. Billy had a look. 'Ooooooooh,' he said. 'Sharp!'

Fierce Milly reached in for them. She lifted them out slowly and held them up.

'Hah!' I said. 'Hallowe'en teeth! For dressing up! They're false false teeth.'

'My granny's not a real vampire?'

'Doesn't sleep upside down. Doesn't fly out windows,' Billy said.

Fierce Milly looked so disappointed.

'Never mind,' I said. 'The teeth look nearly real.'

'I remember!' Fierce Milly said. 'Last Hallowe'en, when I dressed up as a spider, my granny dressed up as a vampire and we frightened the trick-or-treaters. She said that was more fun, and I got all the nuts. I'm going to try these teeth on,' Fierce Milly said.

She jammed them into her mouth, and tried to look in the mirror to scare herself, only it was too high. So she climbed up on her granny's rocking chair. It wobbled, it rocked, it tipped the other way. Fierce Milly stood there like a vampire circus lady on the back of a horse.

'Look at me,' she yelled,

and she made the rocking chair buck and sway again. It gave a little jump on the floor. She made it rock faster and faster. It hopped across the floor. Bump, bump, bump.

'Is she supposed to do that?' Billy asked.

Then the rocking chair chucked Fierce Milly right out of the open window. Everyone screamed, especially Fierce Milly.

Her granny came charging into the room, very fast for a granny, and we all leaned out of the window to see where Fierce Milly had gone. She was lying in a flower bed, howling very loudly.

'The howling's a good sign,' her granny

said. We dashed down and got Fierce Milly out of the flower bed while her granny got her motorbike from the shed and put a big helmet on Fierce Milly, and closed the visor right down so the howling wasn't so loud, and made her sit in the little sidecar. Then they drove off superfast to the hospital and me and Billy went home. Billy made me pretend to be a motorbike. He held on to my pocket and ran alongside me, so he could be a sidecar.

'I wish our granny was a vampire so she

could have a motorbike too,' Billy said.

I didn't even try to explain. I was busy making motorbike noises.

The next morning Fierce Milly and Yo-yo Ferguson called for us to go to school. Her arm was in a plaster in a sling and she looked really sad.

'What's the matter?' Billy asked. 'Does your arm hurt?'

'No,' Fierce Milly said. 'It's pink!' And she showed us the plaster. It was very very pink. 'I can't swank around with a pink plaster.'

Fierce Milly hates pink. She's been trying to lose her new pink cardigan for weeks, but people keep finding it and bringing it back. She left it on a bus. She put it on a dog she met in the park. She even left

it away up high in a tree in the Old Man's garden, but he got it down. He must have thrown sticks at it.

'You'll not be able to lose that,' Billy said. 'It's hard as stone and stuck on tight.'

'I know what to do,' I said. 'We'll put our names on it, that'll cover up some of the pink, *and* you'll have some exciting REAL news for Miss.'

That cheered Fierce Milly up, but we were late at school because she kept stopping to get more names on her pink plaster. She got Tony-in-the-Shop's name, and Mrs McMichael's, and Cecil Nutt's granny's, and the postman's, and the name of a lady who was going past, and even the headmaster's. Billy's name was there ten times in ten different colours of markers. Mine was there, nice and neat, and Yo-yo Ferguson's was there. He must have had help, seeing as he's only a cat. The plaster was turning a sort of yucky grey with all the names. Fierce Milly liked it that way.

'Look at all my autographs, I'm famous.'

Miss was just about to ask if anyone had any exciting but *nice* news when Fierce Milly burst into the classroom, waving the yucky grey plaster in the air. She didn't even wait for Miss to speak. This was Fierce Milly's news:

'I put in my granny's vampire teeth and I rocked my granny's rocking chair so fast that it catapulted me right through the air, and I flew out the window like a real vampire and I hurt my arm and I had to go to the hospital, and I got a plaster in a sling, and I frightened all the doctors and nurses with my vampire teeth and my mum took them off me, and it's all true news, so you have to put it on the board, because here's the evidence.'

She clunked the plastered arm down on Miss's desk, just in case she hadn't noticed it.

'Dear me, Mildred!' Miss said. 'I don't think you should do that with your lovely new plaster. You might break it! I think you should go and sit down, and don't swing it about in the air like that! Duck, Ursula!'

We all ducked and Fierce Milly got safely into her seat, and Miss put her news up on the blackboard. This is what

Miss wrote:

Fierce Milly whispered to me, 'That's so boring it's just not true!'

At breaktime somebody sneaked into the classroom and changed it.

Miss never noticed.

3.
Fierce Milly and the demon saucepan

The next day Miss picked Ursula's news for the blackboard as usual. 'Ursula's mum has six new saucepans. They all fit inside each other. Isn't that nice?'

'Isn't that boring,' Fierce Milly said and she yawned so hard I thought her head would fall off, and everybody else started yawning, because yawning's catching. Even

Miss yawned. Then she got cross.

Miss scolded, 'Saucepans are very useful objects, and I think it is a good idea for us all to think about how useful saucepans are. For story time today, we are all going to write about saucepans, and our stories will be called, "A Day in the Life of a Saucepan".'

Everybody groaned.

'Just pretend you're a saucepan and write down all your adventures.'

Then Fierce Milly got into even more trouble. She pretended to be a saucepan and stuck her arm out straight, to be her handle, to see what it would feel like to have one. But Ursula got in the way of

her handle and said that Fierce Milly had whacked her on the nose deliberately. Fierce Milly had to sit at the back of the classroom all on her own for the rest of the day.

When we called for her after school she was still scolding about Ursula's saucepans. 'I've got to write my rotten old saucepan story so I can't come out to play. I didn't get it done in school. I couldn't even get started. What's there to say about boring saucepans? It's just not fair. I'm going to make an Ursula-disappearing-spell.'

But next morning, on the way to school, Fierce Milly was in a very good mood.

'I got my "Day in the Life of a Saucepan" story finished. It's the longest story ever. It's ten pages long and I kept my writing tiny. Miss will *have* to give me a gold star for it.'

'What happens in your story?' Billy

asked. He should have known better.

'I'll tell you as we go.'

This is some of Fierce Milly's saucepan story:

> *My saucepan is big enough to boil a boy in, and it has been taken over by an evil spirit. It has glow-in-the-dark eyes and it can boil by itself and make clouds of steam like a dragon. If you are in the kitchen at night when it is dark, you can see the*

gleam of the glow-in-the-dark eyes shining out through the crack in the cupboard door, and if it is angry you can see steam puffing out. *It* is always angry . . .

'I don't like that saucepan,' said Billy.

One day Fierce Milly's demon saucepan escaped from the cooker. It whizzed its handle round and round like a helicopter and it flew out the window and dropped hot potatoes on the people below. And when Fierce Milly said in a spooky voice, 'And then it laughed its evil saucepan laugh and whipped its handle around in the air like a tiger's tail . . .' I felt Billy grab my hand.

'Can kettles do that, Susan, or is it only

saucepans?' he asked.

'It's only a story, Billy. It's not real. Are we near the end of this story yet, Fierce Milly?'

'We're only on page two,' she said.

'Don't you dare have any saucepan dreams tonight, Billy,' I said. But by then it was time for us to go off to our classrooms.

The first thing Miss said was, 'Let's listen to some of your "Day in a Life of a Saucepan" stories. Who wants to go first?'

Fierce Milly wanted to go first, of course. She had her story ready, pages and pages of it, and she started reading at once:

'A Day in the Life of a Saucepan by Fierce Milly. Except that my story is really a fortnight in the life of a saucepan. It's the longest story ever, you're going to have to give me a gold

star for it.'

'Well, let's hear it first,' said Miss, and she sat back in her chair, crossed her arms and closed her eyes. She says she does this all-the-better-to-concentrate. She didn't concentrate on Fierce Milly's story for long. When Fierce Milly got to the bit about the demon saucepan flying around and biting people's heads off with its lid, Ursula started to cry, and Miss's eyes flew open as if they were on springs. She said in her loud now-that's-enough-of-that voice. 'Thank you Mildred! I think we'll hear someone else's story now.'

'But what about my gold star? You need to hear the whole story so you know how great it is! Then the saucepan

glowed red hot and sizzled around all over the room . . .'

'Sit down Mildred, please!'

'It melted the Barbie and poured it out in a little puddle of pink plastic, with two Barbie eyes floating on top of it . . .'

'Here's a star! Now please, STOP!'

That's the first time ever anyone got a gold star for stopping a story. Fierce Milly was really pleased.

'Ursula,' Miss said, 'why don't you stop crying and read us your story?'

This was Ursula's story:

'I am a saucepan. I am metal. I live in a cupboard. I sit on a shelf. I have a glass lid.

I have a plastic handle. I come out on the cooker at dinner time. I cook potatoes in me. I cook gravy in me. I cook cabbage in me. I cook . . .'

We all breathed sighs of relief. Sometimes boring is just great. Miss closed her eyes again. All-the-better-to-concentrate.

At breaktime Fierce Milly boasted about getting a gold star just for the beginning of a story. Cecil Nutt said she was making it up about the star, no one would give her a star for one of her rotten old stories. She

said she'd show him and went back into the classroom to get her story, star and all.

She showed it off to Cecil Nutt a wee bit too much. He said he was so impressed he was going to put his name on her plaster. But he didn't write his name. He wrote MILDRED'S SORE ARM in enormous letters and then ran away fast and hid in the boys' toilet.

Everyone knows how much Fierce Milly hates being called Mildred. Only Miss is allowed to do it. We all watched. Fierce Milly might burst. She might explode. She didn't do any of those things. She did something nobody expected. She ran right after Cecil Nutt straight into the boys' toilet! Everyone in the playground was so shocked you could have heard a pin drop.

'She's not supposed to do that,' Billy whispered.

'I know,' I said. 'She'll get in terrible

trouble.' No one who wasn't a boy ever went in the boys' toilets, except for Miss once when someone was stuck. Besides which, everyone knows there's a ghost in the boys' toilets.

Fierce Milly didn't come out, and didn't come out. Neither did Cecil Nutt. We all stood round at a very safe distance.

'Maybe she's flushing him down the toilet!' Billy whispered.

They didn't come out and they didn't come out.

'Maybe the ghost ate them,' said Billy.

'Stop it!' I said. 'You're getting as bad as she is. I'm going to tell her to come out of there before Miss finds out.'

I went just as far as the door. I could hear a spooky voice making strange scary noises. Was that the ghost?

I stepped just inside the door. Nothing happened – yet. I couldn't believe that I was really going into the boys' toilet, but Fierce Milly might be in terrible danger. I peeped round the edge of the door. Then I saw her . . .

I dashed right back to where everyone else was waiting.

'She has Cecil Nutt trapped in the corner by the washhand basins. He's crouching on the floor with his hands over his ears! She's reading him her saucepan story, every last word of it. She won't be out of there for ages. She's only on page two.'

'Poor Cecil!' Billy said.

Fierce Milly didn't come out until break was nearly over. She marched into the playground with a big happy smile on her face, and borrowed someone's pencil to score out the Mildred on her plaster. Then Cecil Nutt staggered out, as pale as a toilet, looking all around him as if he expected something to fly down out of the air. His eyes were as big as saucepan lids.

'Is he looking a bit flushed?' Fierce Milly said, and smirked.

4.

Fierce Milly and the Jumble cat

The next day, Miss said, 'Did you all leave the school letters with your neighbours, asking them to leave out jumble for the school jumble sale? Well, today's jumble collection day and I have really exciting news for you!'

Fierce Milly rolled her eyes and sighed, but it really was exciting news. Whoever got the most jumble would win a surprise prize. Fierce Milly was sure that we would win it, whatever it was. She talked about nothing else all the way home.

'It might be an encyclopaedia,' said Billy, who likes looking things up. Fierce Milly said she thought the prize might be disco lights. I said I'd just wait and see. But Fierce Milly wasn't listening, she kept disco dancing round the pavement.

'I'll have discos in my garage. And I'll get a sparkly frock and no one else will be allowed to dance at my discos, just me, but you can all come and watch, except for Cecil Nutt. I'll put up a big poster outside to say NO NUTTS DISCO.'

'We have to get the most jumble first,' I said.

''Course we will, see you after tea.' And she ran off up the street to her house. 'Eat fast!' she shouted back.

'Something's missing,' Billy said, watching her go . . .

Mum said dinner wasn't ready for ages, go and get an apple. But Billy couldn't stop thinking about dinner, and every time he thought about it he got hungrier and hungrier. An apple wasn't enough.

'Why don't you think about something else?' I said.

'I can't. Besides, it's not me that's thinking about dinner. It's my tummy that's thinking about dinner.'

So Billy took his tummy into the kitchen to see what was happening.

He came out doublefast and ran straight upstairs and right into his bedroom.

'What happened?' I yelled. But he didn't answer. So I went into the kitchen to see.

There was just a big saucepan, bubbling on the cooker. Every so often the lid did a little hop, rattled, and a big squirt of steam hissed out. It was the potatoes, boiling for dinner, but I knew what Billy thought it was and I went off to find him. He was under the blanket.

'You thought it was Fierce Milly's demon saucepan, didn't you? Well, it's not, it's just our spuds cooking for dinner. And that demon saucepan is only made up.'

'I know,' Billy said. 'But it's still scary.'

'I thought your *Mighty Monsters of the Universe* book was making you brave.'

'It is, but only about things that are in it. And there's no demon saucepans in it. I looked.'

'Let's see,' I said. 'There might be something in it a bit like the demon saucepan.'

'There's nothing in the world like the demon saucepan except saucepans,' Billy said.

He reached the *Mighty Monsters of the Universe* out from under the blanket. I looked through it, right to the empty page at the back of the book. No saucepan. Then I had an idea.

'I know how to stop you being frightened of the demon saucepan,' I said. 'Get me your pencils.'

I drew the demon saucepan in the back of Billy's *Mighty Monsters of the Universe* book. I gave it glow-in-the-dark eyes and lots of steam. Then I wrote over the top

of it in big red letters, and underlined it three times:

THIS IS THE DEMON SAUCEPAN. ALL OTHER SAUCEPANS ARE ORDINARY BORING OLD SAUCEPANS.

'Oooooh!' said Billy, all smiles.

Mum called us down for dinner. It was mashed potato volcanoes with melted butter in them and peas and fish fingers. The saucepan was in the sink with its handle sticking up like Yo-yo Ferguson's tail when he's pleased. But Billy didn't mind it one bit. He was busy thinking about his dinner.

'I just knew it would be mashed potato volcanoes!' he said and he made a fish finger fort for his peas and then whacked a potato volcano to let all the melted butter run out.

Fierce Milly called after dinner.

'I know what's missing,' Billy said. 'Where's Yo-yo Ferguson? Why isn't he with you today? Did you make a cat-disappearing spell after all?'

'Did not,' she said. 'He didn't call for me.'

Billy went to get his *Mighty Monsters of the Universe* book.

'Just in case. You never know what might be up our street. I might need to look something up.'

We brought Billy's old pram from when he was a baby, to put all the jumble in. I pushed it because Fierce Milly would only go speeding up the pavement and crash into people. First we went to call for Yo-yo

Ferguson, but Mr Ferguson said he didn't know where Yo-yo was. He'd last seen him sniffing around the jumble. You know how nosey cats are.

'Did you and Yo-yo Ferguson fall out? Is he not speaking to you?' Billy asked.

Fierce Milly looked a bit cross, but she cheered up and forgot about Yo-yo when she saw all the jumble that the Fergusons had left out for us. There was a broken tennis racket and the sucking bit off an old vacuum cleaner and three brand new calendars from last year.

Next was Mrs McMichael's house. She had left out a lovely little ballerina-dog ornament with a real lace sticky-out pink ballet skirt with sparkly sequins on it. Fierce Milly made Billy carry it back to the pram.

'That thing is soooo yeuch!' she said. 'Hide it under Ferguson's calendars.'

I thought it was gorgeous. I wished it were mine.

Tony at the corner shop gave us some toys that he played with when he was little. We were all surprised.

'Did you used to be little?' Billy asked.

Tony told us to get away on out of that or he'd take the toys back. The pram was getting heavier and heavier, and slower and slower. We had

a mountain of jumble. I was glad when we got to the last house. It was the Old Man's house and you can't push a pram up his garden path because it's all blocked by big bushes that make his whole garden dark and scary. Fierce Milly said she'd go for the Old Man's jumble, because she's never scared.

Me and Billy sat on top of the wall and watched the bushes rustle all the way up the garden, right to the top. Then there was a terrible screech and the bushes started to rustle very fast all the way back down the garden.

'That must be her frightening something,' Billy said.

Fierce Milly vaulted over the wall and

leaned up against it, panting, staring. She didn't have any jumble.

She gasped, 'There's something terrible in there, on the doorstep . . . it's horrible, it's awful . . .'

Her eyes were as big as dinner plates. She was pale and trembling.

'Is Fierce Milly really scared?' Billy asked. 'It must be bad then. I'll get my book.'

And before I knew what was happening, Billy had hoicked his *Mighty Monsters of the Universe* book out of the pram, and was away off up the Old Man's garden.

'I don't believe it!' I yelled. 'Come on, Fierce Milly. After him!'

We caught up with Billy just as he reached the top of the Old Man's garden.

'I can't look!' Fierce Milly said.

An old lamp and an enormous saucepan sat on the Old Man's doorstep – jumble. But – I couldn't believe my eyes – the huge saucepan was wobbling. Its lid rattled and bounced. It looked ready to fly in the air, and worst of all – it was yowling like a demon.

Billy just walked up to it and whacked it with his *Mighty Monsters of the Universe* book. The saucepan tipped over. Its lid dropped off, and Yo-yo Ferguson flew out

and ran straight past us, all the way down the garden, right out of the gate.

'I knew it was just an ordinary saucepan. It says so in my book,' Billy said, and he began to gather up the Old Man's jumble.

'And I rescued Yo-yo from being jumble,' he added.

I just knew that Billy was going to go on and on about this.

'I wasn't one bit scared, really,' Fierce Milly said on the way back down the garden. 'I was only pretending.'

Yo-yo Ferguson was sitting in the pram, licking his paws and trying to look as if he had been there all day. We let Billy ride home in the pram, with Yo-yo Ferguson and the jumble. Me and Fierce Milly pushed.

We won the prize for collecting the most jumble. Fierce Milly was right about that, but she was wrong about what the prize would be. It wasn't disco lights. It was the ballerina-dog with the pink sticky-out lace skirt. Fierce Milly said I could have it. It's just gorgeous, so it is. Ursula's jealous.